THE CHANGE

GUY ADAMS

SOLARIS

First published 2017 by Solaris
an imprint of Rebellion Publishing Ltd,
Riverside House, Osney Mead,
Oxford, OX2 0ES, UK

www.solarisbooks.com

ISBN: 978 1 78108 587 5

10 9 8 7 6 5 4 3 2 1

A CIP catalogue record for this book is available
from the British Library.

Designed & typeset by Rebellion Publishing

Printed in the UK

4

LONDON
DIRT

Chapter One

'You should try some,' said Jerome.

'No thanks,' Kirby replied, poking at the campfire. It was a crackling mess of dry packing crates that burned brightly but briefly, like so many things in the world post-Change. 'I've seen what it does to people,' she said. 'Spaced. Stupid. Out of their heads.'

'Well yeah,' said Jerome, 'why take it otherwise?'

He opened the small plastic bag and took out a pinch of the dried leaves, grinding them up on his palm. This stuff had so many names, Kirby could barely keep up with it. Most people seemed to have settled on 'chase', after the rush the stuff gave you.

'Good quality,' he said, feeling the powdered results between his fingers, 'never get it pre-crushed, they mix in all sorts of crap then. Straight leaf. Only way.' He lowered his face to his palm and sniffed the powder.

Kirby wished there was somewhere else she could be than here. Cluttering up a derelict South London street with an idiot for company and nothing to look forward to but a bad meal and broken sleep. She looked into what remained of the glass windows of the discount supermarket they'd camped outside. They reflected the flames of the fire and in the half-light her face stared back at her: crew-cut hair and eyes that held every haunted moment of the last few months.

She'd been on her own for about six weeks before meeting Jerome and the relief of having somebody to share the road with had blinded her to how annoying he was. Pre-Change she hadn't minded her own company but the end of the world makes socialites of us all. Even now, as tempting as it was, she couldn't bring herself to just walk away. She didn't think Jerome would actually miss her; once he'd realised that travelling with her didn't mean she'd share his sleeping bag, his enthusiasm for her company had taken a sharp nosedive. The world as they knew it may have curled up and died but teenage lust was eternal. Still, he was fragile, much more fragile than he liked to pretend, and the idea of abandoning him to the mess of his own stupid self-destruction made her feel bad.

She'd met lots of kids like Jerome. Kids that had taken one look at the world they now lived in and sprinted towards something to soften its edges. They decided they weren't going to make old bones so why worry? If you're going to die then go out with a smile on your face. Kirby didn't think existence was so disposable. It was a miracle she'd survived The Change and to throw it away now would be insane. How many people had survived those few minutes when the sky had filled with impossible creatures? Who knew the number? The number didn't matter. *Most* people had died. Kirby was fifteen years old and a lot of them had been a mixed blessing, pre-Change. That day though, *that day* Kirby had struck it lucky and she didn't believe in throwing luck away.

'So good,' Jerome droned, lying back on the sleeping bag they'd stolen from a camping shop in Camden. 'You can feel it pouring through you like honey.'

Kirby wondered if the food was cooked yet. The sooner she ate, the sooner she could zip herself up in her sleeping bag and ignore Jerome until the morning. She heard the food beginning to bubble.

Using her knife, she carefully lifted off the metal lid of the cooking pot and stirred at the tinned stew inside it. She removed the knife and dabbed the tip of it with her finger. Still only lukewarm. But the sound of it bubbling had been so loud, how could it only be...? She looked at the stew. It wasn't bubbling. It was just sat there in the unappetising gloop of its gelatinous gravy.

So what was that noise?

'Jerome?'

Beyond the fire, the kid had rolled onto his side, his back towards Kirby.

'Jerome?'

Bubble, bubble, pop, hiss...

Kirby got up and moved over to him. The noise she'd thought was their food cooking grew louder the closer she got. There was a dry sound now too, a rustling sound.

'Jerome?'

She reached out, her fingers brushing the back of his greasy hoodie before she'd even noticed the fabric was moving, rippling and shifting as if something was underneath it, trying to get out.

She snatched her hand away.

'Jerome?'

Jerome rolled over of his own accord. No, not his own... because even in the low light of the fire, Kirby knew there was very little of Jerome left in front of her.

The kid's skin was bubbling and splitting as dark, oily shapes pushed their way through. What was that? Worms? Snakes?

The shapes unfurled to reveal runners and leaves, like speeded-up footage of a seed sprouting. The leaves glistened in the light of the fire and Kirby backed away, kicking over the pot of stew so that the contents spilled, hissing, into the hot embers of the fire. Jerome was rising up, forced upright by the growths that were pushing through his flesh. His body twisted, mouth falling open as more foliage poured out, teeth forced aside to scatter on the ground.

Kirby ran.

This wasn't the first time she'd been face-to-face with something grotesque post-Change; every day brought horrors. She'd do what she'd always done: she'd outrun it. She knew, looking back on it, that her obsession with running pre-Change, the hours and hours of training, the strains and the torn ligaments, had been because she had wanted to escape her life at home. It hadn't worked: you couldn't ever run away from your life, you always brought it with you. She was glad of it these days though, every race, every single lap had been perfect training for the new world. She was the lucky kid. She was the survivor. She kicked the empty can the stew had come in and it bounced ahead of her with a clatter, getting a head start.

Behind her she heard the sound of snapping bone as Jerome's body folded in on itself.

She was suddenly bathed in light and the roar of car engines as three vehicles turned into the street.

'Gregor's going wild,' a voice shouted, 'the sproutling must be close.'

Kirby dropped back, shoving herself behind a large dump bin, the street filling with the sound of opening car doors, stamping military boots and the click of automatic weapons. Underneath it all she could hear a high-pitched sound, an inhuman cry of panic.

They were a small crew of nine or ten. All wearing camouflage uniforms and full-face head-masks. Most of them were sweeping the street with searchlights but, at the rear, by the two military vehicles they'd arrived in, Kirby could see a pair of figures holding back a third. That third cast an unusual silhouette, constantly on the move, the unearthly whine coming from somewhere inside it.

'There!' a voice shouted. Several searchlights converged on the writhing fusion of meat and plant that had once been Jerome.

'Rapid change!' someone else shouted. 'Hormone spray! Quickly!'

Kirby pressed herself further back into the shadow of the bin as two soldiers in hazmat suits moved past the others, one holding a large metal canister the other carrying a rifle-shaped spray gun.

'Stand back!' the man with the canister shouted and the chemical was sprayed at high pressure, knocking the flailing Jerome-creature back as it was doused with the liquid. It writhed in the jet, leaves and broken limbs splashing and spraying the chemical against the dirty, smoke-stained wall behind it. Finally it fell forward with a wet squelching noise and the spray was shut off.

Several of the other men came running forward, now dragging a large crate between them. The men in the hazmat suits had put down the spray gun and were dragging the Jerome-creature towards the crate. The lid was popped open with a hiss of escaping air and they dumped the mixture of man and plant inside, picking up trailing tendrils and piling them on top.

'Secure!' one shouted and the lid was replaced.

In the silence, the whining sound of the restrained man was even more pronounced. The soldiers ignored it as they carried the crate back to one of the vehicles and loaded it inside.

There was the crackle of a radio. 'Containment achieved,' said one of the soldiers.

'Excellent,' came the reply over the radio, *'ensure you retrieve any samples of the leaf.'*

Kirby looked over to where one of the other men was holding up the plastic bag of chase Jerome had used. He made an 'OK' sign with his finger and thumb.

'Check that,' the soldier replied, replacing the radio on his belt. 'Everyone out.'

The two soldiers in the hazmat suits hoisted up the chemical canister and the spray gun and began to carry them back towards their transport. As they passed Kirby's hiding place, the soldier carrying the canister, his vision limited thanks to his heavy helmet, stepped on the now empty can of stew and lost his balance. He fell towards the bin Kirby was hiding behind, reaching out a hand to steady himself. He shoved the bin at the wall, crushing Kirby behind it. She cried out as it forced her back against the wall and the next thing she knew she was facing loaded automatic rifles, blinded in the beam of searchlights.

'Looks like we've got another volunteer for Krynter's experiments,' the commanding officer said, a woman's voice. 'Load her in the van, she can ride with Gregor.'

The luck that had kept Kirby alive for fifteen years had finally run out.

Chapter Two

NEXT TIME, HOWARD thought, I'll listen to Hubcap. Burgers are just not worth dying for.

'Faster!' Hubcap shouted, a few metres ahead, 'he's gaining!'

Howard saw the reflection of the man chasing them in the cracked rear-windscreen of a coach. His stained chef's whites, his absurd, torn toque hat like a nuclear mushroom cloud detonating over his red, screaming face. As Howard darted between the lanes of abandoned cars he lost sight of the chef again but he could still hear the man's heavy, bare feet and wheezing breath. Every now and then he would drag his rusted cleaver along the paintwork of the cars, resulting in a high-pitched squeal.

They'd seen this man's roadside van, rocking gently on the side of the road, sweet smoke climbing out of a creaking vent on its roof. Hubcap had been all for giving the van a wide berth but, sick of roadside meals of tinned food, Howard had insisted that it had to be worth a look. He had wondered where the chef got his fresh meat from. They knew now: he got it from the people stupid enough to stop by his van. Which is why both of them were now running as fast as they could, to avoid being minced and fried up with onions.

'Chop chop!' the chef screamed.

'Whatever,' Howard muttered as he ran between a small van and an open top sports car, its upholstery pecked apart by birds, making it look like it had been strafed by bullets.

'Aah!' His foot had caught on something and he fell forward, hitting the ground hard. He looked down and saw what had tripped him: the hooked, skeletal fingers of a corpse that had been lying between the cars.

Howard got to his feet but the chef was already on top of him and he had to duck to avoid the lunatic's cleaver.

He shoved the chef backwards but it was like pushing at a brick wall. A brick wall that was off its head and wanted to remove yours.

'Chop chop!' the chef said again, his mouth salivating so much the words came out sounding like a fart in a bath.

Howard kicked and punched at him, booting the man hard between his legs.

The chef's face ballooned as the man doubled over.

Howard turned to run but the bent-over man swung out with his cleaver, its blade catching in the straps of Howard's backpack. They both fell forward, the huffing lunatic landing on Howard's legs. The cleaver clattered to the road and Howard turned to grab at it but the chef's weight held him down. He felt a sharp pain as the man bit into his thigh. Howard kicked out as hard as he could, trying to pull himself free. The chef's fat, damp fingers grabbed at Howard's backpack, pulling himself on top of him.

'Tasty boy!' the man said, the voice hot in Howard's ear. 'Tender and sweet!'

Suddenly there was a loud, resounding clang and the chef dropped forward, utterly immobile.

Hubcap dropped the length of exhaust pipe he'd used to hit the chef and pulled at the unconscious man until Howard could wriggle free.

'Thanks,' Howard said as he brushed himself down.

Hubcap shrugged. 'No worries. Next time though, you listen to me. That way we can avoid all the annoying running and nearly being dead.'

'Fair enough.'

They moved off, hoping to put enough distance between themselves and the unconscious chef before he woke up.

WHEN THE LIGHT began to fade, they made camp on the edge of a supermarket car park. They were wary of the shop itself having only barely escaped from Brent Cross a few days ago. Mobile sentient scanners had wanted to check their barcodes and were sending anything not on the stock list to the compactor in the basement. If it hadn't been for an unexpected strafe run from the human/plane hybrids infesting the nearby RAF museum they would have both been reduced to small cubes of meat and bone.

Howard still hadn't quite got his head around the landscape post-Change. The pockets of civilisation, like that at the Kingdom of Welcome Break, were one thing; humankind endured, it was terribly good at that. Outside of those camps—and there seemed a good number of them—the world fell into two categories: wasteland or lethal no-go area. As much as they tried to travel through the former, they invariably strayed into the latter.

Howard did his best to keep them informed by tuning into Radio Lydia, a pirate radio station (run, unsurprisingly, by a woman called Lydia) who interspersed music with live updates fed to her from listeners. The Internet was still functional, if patchy, and people used it as a lifeline of information and communication. The news networks had vanished (so many of them had covered the initial appearance of the creatures in the sky that there were few staff left to run them). But the power was still on, at least in the major cities and so the world wasn't completely silent. Now people relied on one another, hooking up over the communications infrastructure that still existed. They'd go online when they could get a charge for their equipment, or use the radio when all they had were batteries. Hubcap was relying on his radio at the moment. He'd managed to charge his iPad a little at Brent Cross, before they'd ended up concentrating on more pressing matters like running for their life, but who knew when they'd next find a power socket they could leech from? Better, he'd decided, to rely on the stockpile of batteries in his pack. He was listening to the radio now, while Howard found something to eat.

'Just had news in of a gang of hungry cyclists operating in Camden,' Lydia said, 'apparently they're eating pedestrians who stray into the cycle lanes so mind your road etiquette. If you're in Ealing you might want to avoid the old studios, apparently old comic actors have come back to life and are looking for cast members to join their lethal productions.'

'Should we tell her about the guy in the burger van?' Howard asked, opening a tin of green beans.

'Already did,' said Hubcap, 'she hasn't mentioned it yet but she probably will.'

Hubcap had become obsessed about having Lydia mention him on the radio. Howard found that funny, the world was in a mess but some people still wanted their moment of fame. Either that or he had a crush on Lydia—Hubcap had a lot of crushes.

'I wonder what she looks like,' Hubcap said, pulling out his sketchpad and doodling.

Howard smiled and poured the beans into a small pan on the portable gas stove.

Hubcap began to draw. 'She sounds blonde,' he decided.

'How can you know someone's hair colour from the sound of their voice?' Howard asked.

Hubcap shrugged. 'I like blondes. If I'm fantasising I may as well go all out.'

HOWARD HAD BEEN dreaming.

As always, his sleep seemed to fill up with strange images, flashes of horror and impossible visions. They felt like memories of events he couldn't remember living the first time but, more often than not, they ended up being warnings from the future. Glimpses of what lay on the road ahead. Which would be fine if he could understand them (or if they contained good advice; a dream of killer barcode machines or cannibal chefs would have saved them a lot of trouble over the last few days). Usually though, they were so bizarre, so sudden, that he was just left with a gut instinct, a sense of which way they should head next.

When he'd first explained them to Hubcap, his friend had seen it as the final proof that Howard was off his head. Then, once the visions had been proven right he'd ended up accepting them, calling them Radio Howard and taking them at face value. He also didn't question Howard when he told them where they should go. He complained about it occasionally, especially when it sounded dangerous, but he'd always follow. That loyalty meant the world to

Howard. No, *more* than the world; after all, the world wasn't worth much these days.

That night, his dreams were full of creaking foliage, rustling leaves, a high-pitched whine and a single name.

'Who's Milo Shandler?' he asked as Hubcap woke up next to him, shocked out of sleep by the sound of a helicopter soaring overhead.

'What's going on?' Hubcap wondered, moving instinctively towards the cover of the trees that lined the car park. Searchlights were roaming across the ground as the helicopter passed. They settled on the store itself and the helicopter descended to land in front of the store entrance.

'Milo Shandler,' said Howard again, ignoring the helicopter. 'Do you know him?'

'Rich bloke,' said Hubcap, 'Pre-Change, used to turn up on the news a fair bit. Friends with the Prime Minister. Didn't ride around in helicopters as far I know.'

The helicopter discharged a small troop of armed men who ran towards the store.

'I dreamed about him,' explained Howard, moving next to Hubcap in the shadows of the trees.

'Oh,' said Hubcap with a knowing tone, 'one of *those* dreams.'

'Think so.'

'Fine, well we'll worry about that later once we know what's going on here.'

Howard nodded. 'I think that Milo Shandler is exactly what's going on here.'

Chapter Three

MILO SHANDLER LOOKED out over the lawns in front of Kew Palace and thought about death.

All through his life, money had been the umbrella that kept the worst of life's rain from falling on him. Disease, boredom, even ageing had been mitigated by the sheer quantity of cash he had to throw at them. Now, while most of the world lay rotting, both the rich and poor, he wondered, not for the first time, how the future looked.

There are some who would see such a pan-global disaster as the great leveller, the sort of extinction event that rendered such distinctions as ethnicity, religion and, yes, bank balance as moot. Shandler took some pleasure from proving that not to be the case. In its purely physical form, money was now redundant. People didn't care for notes and coins, there were no functioning businesses with which to exchange them. In the early days post-Change a few had seen it as an opportunity to get rich, hoarding goods or taking over shops and exchanging supplies at inflated prices but they were the first idiots to go. Most soon found themselves facing people who weren't willing to pay and were happy to clarify as much with a bullet or blunt object. The rest eventually looked at their empty larders and realised they had two choices: starve or try to eat hard currency. Death would not be long in coming either way.

The sensible people—some would say lucky but Shandler refused to believe in such a weak term as "luck"—had looked at what they already possessed and reasoned how it would lead to them possessing even more. Shandler had found the answer easy enough. He owned the most valuable commodity of all: he owned people. When the world stumbled, he had ensured he kept hold of the people he already possessed. He had offered them safety and food in return for their continued service. Now, across all of his properties, he had the support of a loyal militia and stockpiles of those other great post-Change currencies: food and weapons. As long as you had those you would always be a rich man, with those assets you could only build. Milo Shandler had come up with a very good way to do just that.

His phone beeped in his pocket. He looked at the caller ID, Gracie Fforde.

Fforde was, alongside Shandler and a handful of others worldwide, a member of The Hellfire Club. Centuries ago, it had been the name of an elite social club, renowned for debauchery. Today the name signified something simpler: these were the people who would rise up from the fires of this hell on Earth and turn it to their advantage.

He answered the phone. 'Ms Fforde. How are things in New York?'

'Where's our damn sample, Shandler?' she barked, refusing even the briefest hint of small talk. 'I have my people ready to take a look at it.'

'It's on its way,' he replied, resisting the urge to tell this grating woman where she could stick her attitude. 'Should be with you in a few hours. But you need to be patient, we've had a few more sproutlings so I'm limiting production until we iron it out.'

'Who cares about the sproutlings?' she asked. 'The world can take a few more dead people.'

'*I* care about them, Gracie dear,' he replied, knowing full well his patronising tone would infuriate her, 'because the manufacture of chase is all about control and the sproutlings are all about chaos. I'm working on it.'

He hung up, not giving her time to reply (something else that would infuriate her). It suited him to work with her but he loathed the woman.

Inside the house behind him, a walkie-talkie crackled into life.

'Sproutling located. Moving in.'

'SPROUTLING LOCATED,' TEMPLE said, 'moving in.' She clipped the radio back on her belt and waved the rest of her team towards the supermarket entrance.

The automatic doors had been propped open and now the helicopter rotor blades had ceased, the sound of violence inside was clearly audible. Something was pushing over empty shelving units and forcing its way through the debris left by looters.

'Basic formation,' she said, 'hormone spray front and centre, the rest of us provide cover.'

They moved forward.

Chapter Four

'WE SHOULD PROBABLY just pack up and leave them to it,' Hubcap suggested. 'I don't really fancy getting shot tonight.'

'An armed response team though,' said Howard, 'don't you think that's weird? I mean... what are they, police? Soldiers?'

They were creeping along the edge of the car park, keeping to the shadows on the periphery of the streetlights.

'Police?' Hubcap replied. 'You're joking aren't you? We gave up on organised authority months back. Emergency services don't exist anymore.'

'Well, they're pretty tooled-up for a bunch of lads on an evening stroll.'

From inside the supermarket there was the sound of automatic gunfire.

'They do seem to be shopping aggressively,' Hubcap agreed. 'Maybe the bakery counter has run out of fresh doughnuts.'

There was another burst of fire followed by a high-pitched screaming sound coming from the helicopter.

'Oh God,' said Hubcap, 'what have they got in there? Seriously... let's run away now in a really manly and not-at-all-embarrassing way.'

The soldiers reappeared at the entrance, running for the open. Orders were shouted as the sound of crashing from inside the supermarket grew louder. Something of considerable size was in pursuit.

'Grenades!' the leader yelled. 'Quickly before it gets in the open!'

A pair of small, dark objects sailed through the air and into the supermarket foyer. A pulse of light, a roar, and a wave of displaced air and broken glass swept through the car park. Hubcap and Howard, still a good twenty metres away, were knocked back.

'ATR!' the commanding officer shouted.

'But sir, we're too...'

'Now!'

There was a pause, the sound of fire crackling in the entrance of the store, then a whoosh of air as a rocket was fired towards whatever it was inside.

'Down!' someone shouted.

If the explosion from the grenades had been a shock, the rocket was worse. Exploding in the confined space of the supermarket foyer, the displaced air kicked back through the open doorway and actually made the helicopter tilt on its runners, the soldiers rolling on the ground. From inside the helicopter there came the high-pitched whine Howard and Hubcap had heard earlier, followed by a clatter of the door. A shape leaped from the helicopter and came bounding towards them across the car park.

'Gregor!' someone shouted.

'Daniels, Peterson,' the commanding officer shouted, 'fetch him back. The rest of you, fan out and watch that entrance in case the thing's still kicking.'

What it was that might still be "kicking" was unimportant to Howard and Hubcap, their attention fixed on the figure that was running towards them. Silhouetted against the burning supermarket, it appeared to be a man running on all fours but other dark shapes swirled around him as he moved. At first you might think it was loose clothing but then, when you noticed the shapes were all moving in different directions, you realised there was more—or perhaps less—to this than just a man.

'Run!' Hubcap shouted.

Howard didn't need telling but it was the wrong move on both of their parts. Attracted by their fast movement, Gregor increased his pace, a hunting instinct flaring in what remained of his mind. He wailed in that piercing, high voice and loped after them.

'Keep going!' Howard shouted as he heard the thing right behind him. He hit the floor as Gregor collided into him and was suddenly bathed in the odour of compost and sweet rot.

Hubcap couldn't leave his friend behind. He briefly paused, wondering if there was something he could use as a weapon. Coming up with nothing he just ran screaming at the tangle of Howard and Gregor.

Gregor looked up and, for the first time, Hubcap got an impression of his face. It made Hubcap think of the engravings you sometimes saw on old churches. The Green Man – a human face surrounded by leaves with tendrils of foliage running from its nostrils and mouth. Parts of its body, more branches and leaves, seemed to be wrapping themselves around Howard, drawing him into itself, and Hubcap tugged at his friend, wrestling to pull him free.

'Grab him!' shouted a voice, and, all of a sudden, the two soldiers were on them, pulling Gregor back even as Hubcap got Howard free.

'I've got him,' one said, taking Gregor in an arm lock and shouting into his ear. 'Back down soldier!' he said. 'At ease!'

Gregor responded instantly, becoming slack in the soldier's grip.

From the supermarket there was the sound of another grenade but the two soldiers didn't lose focus. 'You two,' said the one not holding Gregor, raising a handgun to cover them, 'are coming with us.'

'We were just camping for the night,' said Hubcap, pointing at the supermarket, 'this is nothing to do with us.'

'It is now, kid,' the soldier said, gesturing towards the helicopter with his gun.

'FOUND SOME FRIENDS?' Temple asked, waving them towards the helicopter without waiting for a reply. There was no sign of life from the supermarket now, just the crackle of flames and the sound of falling debris.

Howard and Hubcap were loaded on-board, crammed in next to the restrained figure of Gregor, and the helicopter lifted off over the burning hulk of the supermarket.

'Better safe than sorry,' Temple said, tapping the pilot

on the arm and pointing at the supermarket. 'Finish it off.'

The pilot nodded, reached for his controls and two air-to-surface missiles streaked from below the nose of the helicopter, a pair of thin contrails trailing behind them.

The pilot banked away and behind them the supermarket ruptured, more flames and debris sailing up into the night sky.

'Take us home,' Temple said.

Chapter Five

HOWARD LOOKED DOWN over the city. It was a patchwork of light and darkness. He wondered if those dark regions were just without power or whether something else, something destructive, had robbed them of their light. Fires dotted the horizon. Some would be accidental, the smallest fire could spread now there was no fire service to deal with it. Others would be intentional, like the burning supermarket they'd left behind. When chaos took over a society some worked to get back to order, others just relished the madness. Which state of mind would win out, he wondered?

The helicopter flight was short. They rose up over the city, banked south and were descending again within minutes onto open lawns.

'Nice place you have here,' muttered Hubcap as he was shoved out of the helicopter and onto the ground.

'You won't think so for long,' said one of the soldiers.

Temple waved at two of the men. 'Take Gregor and these two to the stables.'

'Stables?' Howard asked. 'You have horses?'

'We have livestock, which now includes you two. For however long you last.'

'Nice,' said Hubcap.

They were pushed ahead by the two soldiers, with Gregor being yanked along on a heavy leash behind them. The soldiers were entirely casual, as if this was the sort of dull duty they had to perform all the time. One shared some gum with the other and they talked about the creature in the supermarket.

'Never seen a sproutling grow that fast,' one said. 'Thing was doubling itself every few seconds.'

'Frankenstein's fault,' said the other. 'Whatever he's messing about with he's out of his depth if you ask me.'

'Frankenstein?' Howard asked.

'You'll meet him soon enough,' the soldier shoved him forward. 'Now mind your own business and keep walking.'

The soldiers were quiet after that, as if the act of having

to engage with Howard was too much of an inconvenience to bother with.

'Sorry about this,' said Howard to Hubcap.

Hubcap shrugged. 'Mate, I'm used to it. Travelling with you mainly includes running and having stuff try to kill you. In fairness, walking anywhere these days is like that, now I just get to do it in company. I have to say though,' he nodded towards Gregor, 'don't fancy yours much.'

'Any idea where this is?' Howard asked.

'Reckon it's Kew Gardens, came here with the school once. Loads of greenhouses and plants and that. Old people drinking tea and eating cake.'

'Not somewhere you'd expect to find a private army then.'

'Not unless the daffodils have turned violent. There's a walk you can take that's built up on stilts, that's good, takes you through the tops of the trees.'

The soldiers led them through the gardens. In the distance they could see the Temperate House.

'As greenhouses go,' said Hubcap, pointing towards it, 'it's pretty big.'

'And occupied,' said one of the soldiers.

The other one laughed but neither saw fit to elaborate.

They arrived at a section of the gardens that had obviously once been where the real work was done, a complex of outbuildings, petrol pumps and waste bins. The soldiers led them to the largest of the buildings, unlocked the main door and shoved them inside.

They found themselves in a central corridor with locked rooms leading off it. At the far end of the corridor, a large window looked out onto the night. The soldiers stopped at the first door on the left, unlocked it and waved for Howard and Hubcap to go in.

'Your room, don't worry if it's not comfortable, you won't be in it long,' one of them said. The other laughed as the door was locked behind them and the soldiers lead Gregor into the room opposite.

Howard and Hubcap's room was stripped of furniture; a plain box with linoleum flooring and a small, barred window that looked out into the trees beyond. The walls were covered with rough graffiti, scrawled names and bored, biological suggestions. Sat in the far corner was a girl dressed in tatty jeans and a heavy parka coat about two sizes too big for her. She stared at them, scratching at her blonde crewcut, then nodded in greeting.

'He's right,' she said, referring to the soldier. 'You won't be here long. I've only been here since last night and I keep hearing them take others. Screaming usually. It'll be our turn soon.'

'Our turn for what?' Howard asked.

She shrugged. 'Who knows? Nothing good. Something to do with chase.'

Howard looked at Hubcap. 'Chase?'

Hubcap shook his head. 'No idea.'

'It's a drug,' the girl said. 'Where've you been hiding?'

'On the edge of the city,' said Hubcap, sitting down next to her, 'a place on the M25, the Kingdom of Welcome Break.'

'Sounds like one of those weird groups.'

'Not really, bikers mostly. Took over a service station and hotel. It was nice.'

'Should have stayed there then,' she snorted.

'That was my fault,' said Howard, sitting down on the opposite side of her and holding out his hand. 'Howard.'

She stared at his hand for a moment. 'Not sure I want to know your name as we're all likely to be dead soon.' She shook it anyway. 'Kirby.'

'You're called Kirby?' laughed Hubcap. 'That's not a girl's name.'

'I'm a girl and it's my name,' she said, staring at him, 'so piss off.'

'Right,' Hubcap nodded, 'sorry. I'm Hubcap.'

She held her stare. 'And you thought taking the mick out of my name was a good idea?'

'Hubcap's a perfectly good name,' he insisted.

'For a wheel trim, not a human being. What's your real name?'

'Hubcap,' he replied, folding his arms and refusing to back down.

'He won't tell anyone,' said Howard, 'so Hubcap it is.'

Kirby shrugged. 'Whatever. I won't have to use it for long.'

'You said this was something to do with a drug?' Howard asked.

'Chase. Yeah. Dried leaves, loads of people have started taking it because it makes you all vague and dreamy. And it's free.'

'Free drugs? That's new,' said Hubcap.

'What's the point in money now?' Kirby replied. 'There's nothing you can buy with it. Your first few bags are free, after that the dealers call in favours. I've never been stupid enough to take any. Not that it's helped my life expectancy much.'

'Why do you think this has something to do with it?' asked Howard.

''Cause the guy I was with took some. Only with him it had some kind of weird reaction. He started... well, he started growing, leaves and stuff sprouting out of him like it was taking over. Then these soldiers turned up, doused him with some sort of spray and dragged both of us back here. I haven't seen him since. I'm glad. He was dead, didn't stop him moving though…'

'That guy that came with us in the chopper,' said Hubcap, 'Gregor. He was half-plant.'

'Not him,' said Kirby. 'He was with the soldiers when they came to get Jerome. I had to ride back here with him. His weird, ugly face staring at me all the way. He whines like a fire alarm. Freaky.'

'That's him,' Howard agreed. 'I think he tried to eat me.'

'In fairness,' said Hubcap, 'that does happen to you a lot.'

GREGOR WAS LOCKED up in his cage and he settled down in the corner to stare up at the moon. His head was a riot of confused impulses. He longed for sunshine and water, his thirst never seemed to end and the strictly rationed bottles the soldiers gave him were never enough. He felt so small, stunted, repressed, he wanted to stretch and expand, to breathe out into his body until it filled the world.

Alongside these basic urges were the memories of the man inside him, Gregor Tobanek. That part of him always seemed to be screaming. It remembered what it had felt like to enlist, the pride of his family, the sense of his becoming more than just the poor Polish immigrant kid, the sense of becoming bigger. He had always dreamed of that – what kid hadn't? – of becoming more than you were. Gregor had achieved that in the cruellest possible way and it haunted his every moment. He wished he could sleep, then at least he might have a few hours a day when he didn't have to be aware of his condition, just a few hours of oblivion. But plants did not sleep.

Gregor stared at the moon and hated it for being so cold.

Chapter Six

SHANDLER STROLLED INTO Krynter's lab to find the man leaning over a large stainless steel operating table, up to his elbows in a mixture of foliage and meat. This was not unusual.

As always when entering the lab, Shandler felt he was in foreign territory. The clutter of sample dishes, bell jars and discarded food wrappers made him feel uncomfortable. This displeased him, he owned this room and everything in it, yet it felt alien. If it wasn't for Krynter's worth he would have the whole building cleared.

Krynter was a short man who had devoted so much of his attention to his own brain that he had little time for anything else. He was overweight, constantly eating while he worked (a half-eaten steak baguette poked out of his lab coat pocket even now, the meat flapping like the tongue of an anaesthetised dog as he moved) and a waft of body odour and fertiliser hung permanently around him.

'It's like he's rotting right in front of you,' one of his lab assistants had been overheard to say. That particular assistant was now doing what Krynter considered the most valuable work of her career by decomposing in the laboratory's compost heap. Krynter may not have cared enough about his personal hygiene to do anything about it but that didn't mean he took insults on the chin. In fact, there was very little Krynter took on the chin; he fought every intrusion, argued every suggestion and had often been known to lash out at his colleagues. The one person he didn't attack, either physically or verbally, was Shandler, because for all his other faults, the one thing Krynter wasn't was stupid.

'Extraordinary propagation rate,' he said to Shandler as he removed his arm from what had once been Jerome. 'I'm having to keep it well dosed to stop it sprouting all over the place. More problems,' he sighed, 'always more problems. To begin with the sproutlings were easily controlled, now…' He looked at the thing on his table. 'If your men hadn't arrived when they did, this thing could have been the size of a tower block given an hour or two.'

'Why is this happening?' Shandler asked.

Krynter shrugged and then realised that was not an answer his employer would accept. 'Plants adapt,' he said, 'it's the way of nature. Perhaps even more so in the case of this one. Bear in mind that the work we're doing here is outside our normal scientific understanding. In fact, it's outside science altogether. The effects of The Change are—and believe me when I say how much I hate to use the word—supernatural. The things we're seeing in the world now don't conform to any scientific laws.' He leaned back against the operating table, and resumed eating his sandwich. 'I am an expert in several horticultural fields but this,' he gestured to the hybrid on the table behind him, 'is not horticulture. It's magic. So I'm limited in my predictions.'

'Not *too* limited I trust?' Shandler asked.

Krynter was only too aware of the inherent trap in the question. If his work was useless to Shandler then so was he.

'I'm your best hope of understanding it,' he replied, 'don't worry. I'm just reminding you that this is all pie in the sky stuff. Even for a genius like me.'

'So predict.'

'Intelligence,' said Krynter, preparing to lick his fingers of steak fat and ketchup then noticing the considerable muck on his hands from Jerome's body. He wiped his hand on his lab coat instead, a five-finger smear from chest to belly. 'The parent plant shows considerable signs of it. To begin with it attacked all comers, yes?'

Shandler thought back to the men who had been shredded within the confines of the Temperate House, their blood sprayed against the glass as they had been torn apart and dragged within the dark earth to rot away as food. 'Yes.'

'But then, after our happy little accident, discovering the effects the plant's leaves had on people, we took cuttings for drying. That was in the plant's best interests, yes? It wants to thrive, to expand. It's like birds eating tree fruits so as to spread the seeds. It's symbiosis.'

'It allowed us to do it.'

'More than that,' said Krynter, 'it encouraged us. Each batch of chase we've produced has been more potent than the last. More invigorating for the consumer and, of course, more addictive. It's altering itself to be more attractive. It's like evolution but from the wrong end.'

Shandler shook his head. 'Explain.'

'In evolution the trees with the tastier fruits were more eaten, their seeds therefore more widely cultivated. Those trees thrived by virtue of the fact that they were attractive.

Trees with low-hanging fruits are the same. But those trees weren't making a conscious decision to impress, it's just natural selection, those best suited to thrive are the ones that flourish. Our plant seems to be acting consciously. So what is its next logical step? To find a way of using the cuttings we take as a way to expand, to self-seed if you like, spread itself further and further...'

The significance of this wasn't lost on Shandler. The importance of chase was simple enough: it was just another way to own people. The more people they got hooked on the drug, the more people they would control. Throughout testing, chase had proved to be a perfect combination: it had very little long-term effect on the user but was lethally addictive. As a way of building a committed, productively viable slave force it was perfect. That's why the rest of The Hellfire Club had been so impressed with his discovery. But if the drug became permanently lethal, current addicts would drop like flies and nobody else would be stupid enough to take it.

'If that's the case then we'll no longer be able to use it,' he said.

Krynter raised his hands as if to say "exactly". 'Which is why I'm doing everything I can to isolate whatever it is that's contaminating more recent batches so we can try

and neutralise it. And I'm getting there. The problem is...
it's changed once, will it do it again? Just how intelligent
is this damned weed?'

In the Temperate House, the subject of Shandler and
Krynter's conversation curled and writhed in the close
atmosphere. Its foliage fluttered in the still, humid air like
the leathery wings of a restless swarm of bats.

They had wondered on this plant's intelligence.
Wondered how much of a mind it possessed. Somewhere,
in that mass of stalks, branches and foliage did a
rudimentary brain exist? In truth it had only one drive,
only one "thought". It wanted what all living organisms
want: it wanted to *thrive*.

Krynter had been so self-satisfied when he'd managed
to use a hormone spray pumped through the sprinkler
system to limit the foliage growth of the voracious plant. It
hadn't stopped it altogether of course, that wouldn't have
served anybody's purpose. It had, however, seen them limit
the growth to an amount they could control, creating a
replicating source that would renew after daily harvesting.
Once he'd got the balance right, Shandler's men had been
able to cut a few hundred kilos of the plant a day, only

to find the same quantity available to them again by the following morning. Perfect balance.

But Krynter had ignored one vitally important detail: a plant doesn't only grow above ground. Beneath the earth, deep in the compacted darkness of dirt and stone, unaffected by the hormone spray, its roots pushed forward, expanding further and further.

IN THE STABLES, the soldiers were fetching another "volunteer" for Krynter's experiments. The young man shouted and fought every inch of the way until he was finally dragged out and silence fell in the building once more.

'What do you think they want us for?' Howard asked.

'By the time we find out it'll be too late,' said Kirby. 'You hear them take people but you never hear them bring any back. Whatever they are doing gets through bodies fast.'

THE CONVERSATION WITH Krynter had shaken Shandler. He could feel his latest business operation crumbling down around his ears and it infuriated him. The manufacture of chase had been so perfect. A cottage industry, certainly, there was only so much he could do with the limited resources, but once his doped-up army had expanded he'd had plans for cultivating several factories all over the country. More parent plants, all being harvested for their leaves until he had a veritable empire on his hands. Not everyone would take the drug to begin with of course, but once supply dropped he could easily have looked to force-feeding those who had been reluctant. Let it spread and spread until he had a sizeable percentage of the current population under his control. Replicate that worldwide via his Hellfire Club connections and a new world order would have been in place within a matter of months. From there he could have forced his addicts to expand into all sorts of other areas, force them into the danger zones to clear out the absurd monstrosities that festered there (a suicidal act that even his own men were reluctant to perform). He could have got everything back under control within a couple of years. Chaos was bad for business.

But now?

His phone bleeped again and he was tempted to ignore it. It was likely to be Fforde and he certainly wasn't in the mood to deal with her. Right now he'd say something that would sour the relationship to the point it would no longer be viable. He glanced at the screen, it wasn't Fforde. It was

HA/HA the strange AI that had become the dominant force in Japan. Dealing with HA/HA was even worse than dealing with Fforde; he couldn't get used to having a conversation with a piece of software, however sentient it had become. Still, he couldn't ignore it, the way things were going, he'd have to talk to all of the Club members and ensure they didn't progress with plans to use chase. They could be developing the next greatest threat to mankind rather than the useful control method they'd planned.

'Konnichiwa, HA/HA,' he said, 'I hope you're having a better day than I am.'

'You are/have been experiencing problems with chase, yes?' the strange, electronic voice asked. 'Algorithms predict catastrophic results within minimal time frame.'

'Do they now?' Shandler did so hate being lectured by a machine.

'Self warned against use,' HA/HA continued, 'self takes no pleasure from being right.'

'"Self" takes no pleasure from anything I suspect. Who told you about the problems with chase? Has Fforde been talking?'

'Gracie Fforde will soon have problems of its own,' HA/HA said, not really answering the question. 'Self also predicted this but few listen to self.'

'We do like to make our own decisions.'

'Decisions based on erroneous data prediction. You would be better to listen to algorithmic results and do as self suggests.'

'You're probably right. For what it's worth, we are having problems with the chase, yes. It seems to be altering its genetic makeup, becoming unreliable and dangerous.'

'Self would suggest it is becoming more like human then,' HA/HA said. Shandler wondered if this was supposed to be a joke. You never could tell with HA/HA. 'Self suggests very strongly you destroy all samples of chase and parent matter now. Failure to do so within the next one hundred and thirty-six minutes will result in unfeasible situation.'

Unfeasible situation? What the hell was that supposed to mean?

'I'll consider your advice.'

'Prediction: you will not do as self suggests.'

'I'll consider it,' Shandler sighed. 'Destroying everything seems somewhat drastic. We're working to control the situation. I don't have to tell you how much time and effort's gone into this.'

'One hundred and thirty-five minutes and counting.'

'And what happens after that?' Shandler was becoming

angry now, he had more important things to do than be given vague threats by an artificial intelligence. 'What if I destroy everything after two hundred minutes, eh? What will that do for your predictions.'

'You do not understand. If you do not destroy everything within the time frame suggested you will no longer be able to destroy anything.'

'And why's that?'

'Self despairs of explaining to illogical processing systems. If you do not destroy all of the plant matter within the time frame indicated it is you who will be destroyed.'

KRYNTER SMILED AT his next lab rat as he bound the young man to a gurney.

'It's all so frustratingly hit and miss I'm afraid,' he said, adopting the sort of casual tone one might use when discussing weather. 'We tweak and we tweak and we hope for the best. On the plus side: if it kills you, at least you'll go out smiling.'

This had little positive effect on the young man in front of him. In fact, Krynter was quite sure the boy would have been screaming were it not for the heavy, leather gag he'd just strapped around his mouth.

Some people just couldn't think positively.

He injected the latest solution of chase and sat back with a bag of pork scratchings to see what effect it would have.

Initially, the boy's body slackened, the mild euphoria coursing through his system and making him docile.

'Good, good,' muttered Krynter, 'now just stay that way, damn you.'

For a moment it looked as though Krynter would get his wish. Then, suddenly, violently, the body began to thrash. The skin rippled with what might have been veins up until the point they burst from the surface, sprouting forth in an explosion of leaf and meat.

'Oh balls,' said Krynter, striding over and stabbing a large syringe into the quivering body. As he emptied the contents of the syringe, the convulsing lessened and finally stopped, limp tendrils sagging to the floor. Krynter sprayed the body with a high dose of hormone chemical, unfastened the securing straps and tipped the gurney contents into a large plastic crate. He topped up the crate with more chemicals and pressed his intercom on the wall by the main door.

'One more for the compost heap,' he said, 'quick as you like.'

He settled back to finish his pork scratchings, ticking off

the batch number he'd just tested. A pair of soldiers came in and dragged the crate out.

'Tweak,' he said, barely even noticing them, 'tweak, tweak and tweak again...'

Chapter Seven

'You ever wonder whether we'd have been better out there?' Brandon asked, hoisting his end of the packing crate that held the remnants of Krynter's experiment. 'I think we'd have been better.'

'Out where?' Marcus asked, grunting with effort and trying to not to trip up. Brandon always made him go in front and once he'd stumbled and ended up swamped by the rotting remains of a test subject. He'd had to shower for an hour.

'You know,' said Brandon, gesturing vaguely with his head, 'not here. Out in the world with the rest of 'em.'

'What?' Marcus snorted. 'Sleeping rough? Hunting for food? Getting killed by all the weird? No thanks.'

'At least then we'd have been our own boss,' said

Brandon. 'Besides, lugging stuff like this around, who's to say we're not going to end up dead anyway?'

'It's harmless.'

'You hope.'

They skirted the Palm House, dropping the crate for a breather while Brandon rolled a cigarette.

'You wouldn't get that out there,' said Marcus.

'Get what?'

'Tobacco.'

'Course I would, loads of stuff left isn't there? It's all just lying around these days. With most of the people dead there's no shortages.'

Marcus shook his head. 'I was on my own for a fortnight before I hooked up with you lot and I tell you, it ain't as easy as you think. People are stockpiling all over the place. Buildings destroyed, supplies gone. Not as if stuff's being shipped in much anymore either is it?'

'Shandler's still transporting stuff, how do you think we distribute the chase?'

'It's all private though isn't it? Those with the resources looking after themselves. If you were just the bloke on the street, all you've got is your own power. You're not on the supply chain anymore. You're just lost.'

Brandon shrugged. 'Maybe. I just don't like all this,' he gestured at the packing crate. 'Sooner or later it's going to bite us on the arse.'

'Not if you keep sitting on it.' Marcus went to lift the crate. 'Come on, let's just get it over and done with.'

They moved on, heading across the lawns and through the trees to the large, fenced-off area that was now designated the compost heap. Pylons surrounded the compound. The pylons supported floodlights and a watering system that sprayed regular doses of chemicals on the heap, designed to break down the plant samples before they got too unruly. What that left were mounds of gently stirring vegetable matter, burping foul gas and shifting from side to side like a field of sleeping elephants. Sometimes, in its ever-changing state, it adopted forms that seemed humanoid, a stretching arm, a howling mouth, but for the most part it was unrecognisable. A stew of living matter.

'I don't know why they don't just incinerate the lot,' said Brandon. 'See? That's the sort of woolly thinking that's going to get us dead one day. Mark my words.'

'Frankenstein still uses them for samples though doesn't he?' said Marcus, calling Krynter by the nickname he'd earned from most of the soldiers. 'I've had to stand guard over him while he does it.'

'Samples,' Brandon spat the word out as if it was a curse. 'Messing about with stuff they shouldn't be messing about with. It'll end in tears. Mine probably.'

They placed the crate on the ground while Marcus unhooked a spray canister from its hook by the main gate. 'You open up, I'll spray,' he told Brandon.

Brandon nodded, unfastened the padlock and unbolted the gate. Marcus stepped past him and began spraying the chemical in a wide arc. The piles of vegetation curled and stirred, shifting like disturbed serpents as the spray hit them. Marcus and Brandon went back for the crate, dragged it inside and tipped out the contents. The remains of David Massey—a young man who, pre-Change had once, proudly, won a place on his school's football team; had kissed Samantha Foley, a girl he'd adored in silence for months; and had just started to foster dreams of becoming a marine biologist—slopped onto the ground. It retained some of its human shape, four limbs, a bulky, bloated torso and an undersized nub of a head, but it was no longer David Massey. David Massey was a concept that no longer existed, gone forever with nobody alive who even remembered him.

'God but it's ugly,' said Brandon, kicking at the writhing form. 'I hope I never end up looking like that.'

'Leave it alone and let's get out of here,' Marcus replied, closing the crate and carrying it back outside the compound.

He turned to look at his colleague. 'You coming or what?'

Brandon stared at Marcus, a fearful look on his face. 'It's got my foot.' He tugged, trying to free himself from the green mass that was flowing over his boot.

Marcus picked up the chemical spray and directed the hose at Brandon's foot.

'Does that stuff burn?' asked Marcus.

'Who cares? It's got to be better than just letting the thing swallow you up.'

'Yes. God yes. Spray it.'

Marcus did so but the chemical seemed to have little effect on either Brandon's leg or the creature that was now halfway up it.

'Do something!' Brandon screamed. 'Before it gets any higher'

Do something? Marcus wondered. Like what? Whatever Frankenstein had done to this last one had clearly increased its resistance to the chemical. An accident, sure, but that wasn't much consolation right now was it?

'Quickly!' screamed Brandon, falling backwards as the green was now halfway up his thigh.

'I'm thinking,' said Marcus, aware that the "legs" of the creature were now elongating, making their way towards him.

'Think quicker!' Brandon cried, pointing his gun at the body of the thing that was attacking him and putting a few bullets in it, as hopeless as he knew they'd be.

'Sorry Brandon,' Marcus said, staring at the tendrils that were now only inches away from his own feet. He turned and ran out of the compound, locking the gate behind him.

'What are you doing?' Brandon screamed.

'The only thing I can,' Marcus replied, 'sorry.'

He tried to ignore the sound of Brandon's screaming as he ran, shouting into his radio. After a few seconds there was no need, the last few cries stifled away into muffled silence.

GREGOR STIFFENED IN his cell, the voice in his head suddenly so dominating, so clear, that it was as if someone had wired a loudspeaker directly into his brain. Every green inch of him bristled as something, some deep primal connection, fizzed through him. Outside, the Mother/Father was electric, something had changed, something great, some new potential... Gregor couldn't understand it, couldn't know it, but he felt the change. It wasn't an emotion, nothing so human as joy or excitement, it was just a sudden positive wave. A hunger perhaps... yes, now he thought about it, it felt like hunger.

Chapter Eight

'HERE'S WHAT I think we should do,' said Hubcap, not for the first time. He'd already been scraping at the walls and trying to pick the lock with the clasp pin on his belt; it hadn't got them anywhere but he was certainly giving it his all.

'There's nothing we can do,' interrupted Kirby, 'we're walking dead and that's that.'

'If that's that then you've nothing to lose have you?' Hubcap said with a smile. 'You may as well just agree to my brilliant idea.'

She just stared at him, having already decided that Hubcap's breed of enthusiasm mixed with sarcasm was bordering on poisonous.

'What's your brilliant idea?' asked Howard, because nobody else was going to.

'It's simple,' said Hubcap, 'which is why it's so brilliant. All the best ideas are simple. We can't open the door, right?'

'Right,' Howard agreed.

'Who are the only people who can?'

'The soldiers,' said Kirby, deciding that the sooner she got his idea out of him the sooner she could ignore it.

'The soldiers! So what we do is wait for them to come and open the door, which our new friend Kirby says is bound to happen soon...'

'Not your friend,' Kirby said.

'Whatever. You will be, we're brilliant. When they come and open the door there are three of us to only two of them.'

'Two of them with guns,' Howard pointed out.

'They don't want to shoot us,' Hubcap said, 'they need us for something. So we just rush at them, really fast, knock 'em over, knock 'em out, and get out of here.'

There was an awkward silence that Howard eventually broke.

'It's not that brilliant, as plans go.'

'Have you got a more brilliant one?' Hubcap asked.

'No,' Howard admitted.

'It's a stupid idea,' said Kirby.

'More stupid than sitting here waiting to die without

trying anything at all?' Hubcap asked her. 'Because that seems *really* stupid to me. I mean, if I'm going to die anyway I'll try anything before giving up. If I thought stripping off and dancing in front of them would help I'd be naked like a shot.'

'Please don't,' said Kirby. 'I'm depressed enough.'

'She's just horrible,' Hubcap said to Howard. 'Don't you think she's horrible?'

'I suppose we may as well try,' Howard said, ignoring Hubcap's question. 'Like you say, it's better than just doing nothing.'

'Right!' Hubcap smiled. 'At least one of you has some sense.' He turned towards the door and adopted a running start position. 'Any time now then...'

They waited.

Chapter Nine

BENEATH THE COMPOST heap, thin roots were curving up towards the surface. Above ground, the thing that had once been David Massey was multiplying at a terrifying rate. Once its initial host was consumed it began feeding on the other rejects. They gave themselves willingly, knowing that the cultivation of this immune sproutling served the greater good. They tore themselves apart and flung themselves into its expanding mass. The air was filled with the sound of crunching and the gentle hiss of the sprinkler system which splashed on the prime sproutling's back with no more effect than a gentle spring rain.

While it might have been stretching a point to call the plant clever, self-preservation is a great whetting stone on which to sharpen intelligence. By the time the soldiers returned in force it had paused in its feeding, curled dormant throughout the compost heap, mimicking the piles of indolent matter that had always lain there.

'ALL LOOKS SECURE to me,' said Temple. She gave Marcus a look that suggested he was full of it. Maybe he'd killed Brandon himself and was now covering his tracks. She wouldn't put that past some of the men under her command, though Marcus had always seemed more of a team player.

'Tell that to Brandon, sir,' said Marcus peering through the fence.

The floodlights seemed to allow for no deception, everything was as it should be.

'He got stupid and paid the price,' said Temple, shouting an order to "stand down" into her radio. 'You know how lethal these things are unless handled carefully.'

'Not once Frankenstein has dosed them,' Marcus replied, 'not usually.'

'If he heard you call him that you'd end up in there yourself,' Temple said, waving the small company of men back towards the barracks. 'Nothing to see, return to your duties,' she told them. 'Get your rest in, I want you sharp when I need you.'

Marcus continued to stare through the fence. 'They don't normally give us any trouble,' he said, entirely to himself by that point.

He thought about the conversation he'd had with Brandon. Maybe they were sitting on a bomb that had already begun its countdown. Maybe they would have been better on the outside after all...

KRYNTER WAS FAILING and he knew it. There was only so long he could keep pretending that his experiments were worthwhile. Eventually, when he proved himself worthless to Shandler, his life expectancy would be as fragile as that of his test subjects.

He should get out. Yes, that's what he should do, run out into the night and never look back. But would he survive out there? He was under no illusions that he was a man of action, he could barely fight genetics let alone human beings. How long would he last in a world that had grown such sharp teeth?

He wished he knew what to do.

He'd thought that his plan of minutely altering the construction of chase and then testing its effects would buy him plenty of time. After all, how many test subjects could Shandler get his hands on? A great deal it turned out. So what had started as a logical, scientific step—albeit one borne out of a desire to play for time rather than any great hope of success—had turned into an endless slaughter that had seen Krynter no further forward and a compost heap that was growing at a terrifying rate.

He didn't mind the deaths. Life was cheap, every scientist knew that, all it took was fertilisation and a little time. But he did mind the monotony of it all, and the certain, inescapable fact that Shandler's patience would wear out before his supply of livestock did.

One more, he decided, one more test and then he'd pack it all in for the night. He knew Shandler wanted him working all his waking hours but a man needed his rest. Maybe tomorrow a new plan would present itself.

He tapped on the intercom. After a few seconds, Temple's voice came through the speaker.

'Another?' she asked, sounding as tired of it all as he was.

'Another,' he agreed. He heard her order two of her men to fetch someone. 'Did I hear some running around earlier?' he asked, before she'd cut the line.

'False alarm, though I was going to talk to you about it. One of the grunts got careless dumping your last,' it was clear that she struggled for the right word, 'remains. Apparently it turned on him. You may want to up the strength of your knockout solution.'

'I find that hard to believe,' Krynter admitted. 'It attacked him?'

'According to his partner, yeah. Grabbed his foot and then swallowed the rest.'

That wasn't right, thought Krynter. None of the failed experiments had shown that sort of mobility after he'd dosed them. Would this damned plant not stop changing for a moment? 'I should probably take a look,' he said. 'Just in case.'

'We checked it out, there was nothing to see, just rot and silence. You know, normal.'

'Nonetheless,' he said, 'I need to check.'

'I'll secure you a couple of men.'

'No need.' As much as he liked the idea of bodyguards he was worried what he might find. If there was something wrong, better he was the only one to know about it for now. It would be easier to run if he wasn't trapped in the middle of a base-wide panic. 'I can manage on my own.'

'You want me to put a hold on your next subject?'

'No, just have it brought in here and strapped down, I'll get to it soon enough.'

*　　*　　*

'WELL, YEAH,' SAID Hubcap as the two soldiers carried him along the corridor like he was a roll of awkwardly wriggling carpet, 'maybe it wasn't such a brilliant plan after all.'

The three of them had been ready, even Kirby for all her reluctance. The minute they'd heard the guards' boots making their way along the corridor, they'd been on their feet and ready to charge the door. If it hadn't been for the fact that the guards stepped back from the doorway they might even have achieved something. As it was they just ended up running screaming into the corridor and the calm aim of two handguns.

'Back inside,' one of the guards had said, the moment well and truly passed for fighting back. 'Except you,' he'd continued, grabbing Hubcap by the scruff of the neck.

Howard had tried again then, anything but see his friend dragged away. He'd charged at the soldier and received a blow to the side of his head that sent him spinning back into their cell. By the time he was back on his feet, the door was locked and Hubcap was gone.

'We tried,' said Kirby, the distraught look on Howard's face enough to break through her coldness.

'I can't lose him,' said Howard, 'I need him.'

'You'll be with him soon enough,' she said, having enough diplomacy not to elaborate.

TEMPLE CUT OFF the intercom and passed a pleasant few moments imagining shooting Krynter. She found the man loathsome on every conceivable level. From the way he looked at her when she walked into his laboratory to the way he referred to his test subjects as "it". He wasn't the only one to dehumanise them, of course, she'd done it herself, referring to them as "cattle" or "livestock". It made it easier to take them to their slaughter. Still, when Krynter did it it was because he truly didn't care, human lives meant nothing to him.

For all Temple brushed it off, especially in front of the men, she knew you should own your actions; if you're taking a human being to be experimented on—because that's what you're being paid to do and, someone, somewhere, has promised you it was for a good reason— then accept the fact, admit it to yourself. People that hid the truth of their actions, or ignored them entirely, were people that would eventually break because, sooner or later, you were going to have to admit what you were.

Temple knew what she was. She might not be proud of it but she could *live* with it and that's all that mattered these days: living. Unlike a lot of the private soldiers her background was trained army and she'd watched all of her platoon die in the first weeks of The Change, during that thin window of stupidity where those in power (the few of them left living) had thought there was something to fight and win. They had soon learned. Fighting the forces of The Change was as productive as opening fire on a storm cloud. Now she was secure, well-fed and respected by the men under her command. Some of them had needed the rough edges knocking off them, some of them had needed slapping into line but she'd made something of them and, so far, had kept most of them alive.

So far.

The sound of panic in Krynter's voice when she'd told him about Brandon... their resident scientist was spooked and that spooked her in turn. Maybe she should keep an eye on Frankenstein.

IN THE LOOSE topsoil of the compost heap, the thin tendrils of the parent plant finally broke the surface and wormed their way inside the scattered mass of what once been

David Massey. Connection was made and the genetic code passed from child to parent in a way that would have made Mother Nature despair had she not already packed up shop and abandoned the world months ago. Immunity was understood. Immunity was shared. Immunity was gained.

A sole branch pushed through the fine gaps in the fence, curling towards the small generator that powered the lights and sprinkler system. Normally, any growth that breached the fence would be cut and burned, it was someone's job twice a day to circle the compost heap on the off chance of just such a thing happening. Still, it wasn't a major priority, because the one thing nobody had given thought to was that the plant might have a basic intelligence, an ability to reason and plan. It twisted around the wiring that lead from the generator to the pylons, tightened and pulled. The compost heap was in darkness.

Now the growing could really begin.

Chapter Ten

KRYNTER HAD LOADED up a satchel of sampling equipment and a large water pistol filled with the strongest mixture of hormone spray he had been able to manufacture. If what Temple had told him meant what he feared, then it would be of little use, but only an idiot assumed in science, especially when their life was at stake.

He moved quietly through the gardens, the brightly-lit compost heap directly ahead of him, the glare of the powerful arc lights visible from everywhere in the grounds. Then the lights turned off.

GREGOR HOWLED IN the darkness, what remained of his humanity desperately trying to refuse the primal commands coursing through him. He burned with it, every part of him being pulled in different directions. He began to shake, his body swelling as the urge to grow could no longer be denied. The pain was impossible for the human part of Gregor to bear as the green both compressed and stretched different parts of his body, forcing him to make the final change, to let go of the fragile history of his species and become something entirely new.

He pressed against the bars and they began to bend, rivets popping. With a loud clatter one wall of the cage fell outward and Gregor threw himself at the wall of the room, desperate to beat and smash away the feelings inside him. He pounded and pounded, his body still enlarging until eventually even the wall could no longer contain him and he spilled over into the corridor outside.

'WHAT THE HELL was that?' Kirby wondered, getting to her feet and moving over to the door. 'Something's seriously wrong out there.'

Howard came up beside her. 'Something attacking?' he wondered as they listened to the inhuman screams and the sound of toppling masonry.

'Just what we needed to make our night even better.'

The wall of their room shook, dry paint and plaster showering down from the ceiling.

'Get back,' Howard shouted as the wall shook once more and a crack worked its way right across it. The door popped in its frame, twisting and falling into the room.

'Come on!' he said, running for the opening.

'Out there?' she asked. 'With whatever's doing that?'

'You'd rather be trapped in here with it?'

She could see the sense in that and they both stepped out into the corridor, coming face to... well, Gregor no longer really had a face. Like the rest of him it was in a constant state of flux, his head expanding and contorting, his mouth a wide hole filled with thrashing foliage and the sounds of agony.

'Look at it,' said Kirby. 'What's happened to him?'

'I don't know,' said Howard, reminded of his dream, of the violence of plants.

Kirby ran towards the other end of the corridor.

'Where are you going?' Howard asked, backing away from Gregor as he continued to grow, the wall of their room finally caving in to allow another portion of him to spill into the space.

'It's between us and the door, stupid,' said Kirby, beating at the window at the end of the corridor. 'So this is our only way out.'

Howard suddenly became aware of the sound of raised voices from other rooms, the other imprisoned test subjects panicked by the commotion.

'What about everyone else?' he asked, pulling uselessly at the locked doors.

'You got keys?' she asked having dashed back to pick up a piece of dropped masonry.

'Of course not!'

'Then there's nothing you can do is there?'

She used the masonry as a hammer, smashing the glass and knocking the remaining shards out of the frame so they had room to climb out.

'We can't just leave them!' Howard stared at Gregor, a green wall of screaming vegetation that filled every inch of available space and was still growing.

'Maybe they'll be lucky like us,' said Kirby, grabbing him by the shoulder and dragging him back to the window. 'But there's nothing we can do about it. Either we run or we stay here and die.'

She was right. He knew that she was right, but, as he climbed out of the window and dropped down to the ground on the other side the sound of panicked shouting from the rooms along the corridor came along with him.

Chapter Eleven

"ONE HUNDRED AND thirty five minutes and counting." That's what HA/HA had said. Shandler had looked at his watch at the time, hadn't been able to help it. It had been thirty seven minutes past seven which placed the AI's deadline at eight minutes to ten. The maths had been quick, the instinctive addition of a man who had spent his whole life conducting meetings, making appointments, ruling his day with a stopwatch. Eight minutes to ten.

He'd tried not to look at his watch since. To put the ridiculous warning from his mind. HA/HA was probably just trying to make him panic. It had been the only member of The Hellfire Club to refuse involvement in his schemes for chase, claiming that it had its own methods for governing its populace. It was jealous that was all, or whatever an AI had instead of jealousy... a programmed drive to be more successful than the competition probably. That was it, it had looked at his plans and recognised their worth. It had realised that it couldn't compete with such a plan. Instead of going back on its original decision and agreeing to try to propagate chase on its own shores it was now hoping to put him off. It wanted him to fail rather than admit its own mistakes. Stupid computer.

He looked at his watch. Ten minutes past nine. Forty two minutes to go. No. He wouldn't think like that, he wouldn't give in to the paranoia the AI was determined to cultivate.

He'd just check and make sure everything was secure though, because that was common sense.

He pressed a button on his intercom, wanting to raise Temple in the barracks. There was silence. He pressed it again, still nothing. What was the woman doing? Had there been another sproutling outbreak and Krynter hadn't thought to inform him? He pressed it one more time and if he didn't get an answer he'd raise her on the walkie-talkie.

'Hello?' came a man's voice he didn't recognise. 'Private Lockley here, who's that?'

'The man who keeps you clothed and fed, damn you,' he shouted. 'Where's Temple?'

There was a slight pause as Private Lockley no doubt panicked at the other end of the intercom line. 'Erm...' the man said, trying to instil an air of authority into his voice and failing completely, 'sorry about that sir. The sarge isn't here, I'm not sure where she's gone. If you give me a minute I'll ask one of the...'

Shandler cut the intercom; he had no intention of being kept waiting by the irritatingly ineffectual Private Lockley. Instead he pressed the intercom button that would connect him with the lab and Krynter. There was no reply. He held his finger on the button, knowing the call alarm on the other end would be blaring out one endless noise.

'For God's sake!' he shouted, after there was still no reply, beating at the wall next to the intercom with his fist. Where were they?

He picked up his walkie-talkie and tried to raise Temple. He got dead air for his efforts.

He looked at his watch. Thirty-eight minutes to go.

TEMPLE HAD FOLLOWED Krynter as the man had set out towards the compost heap. It wasn't difficult; the dumpy little scientist crashed through the undergrowth, constantly muttering to himself and she had no doubt that he was completely unaware he had company out there in the dark. She moved quietly, ever a trained soldier, watching where she put her feet and keeping to the shadows. Just because she was dealing with an idiot didn't mean she should forget how things should be done properly.

She was only a few feet behind him when the lights to the compost heap cut out. For a moment, like him, she had just stared at the patch of darkness wondering what the failure meant. Was it a power outage? They looked after the generators well, topping them up regularly; she'd instilled into her men the importance of caring for your equipment. Still, it had to be the likeliest explanation. After all, who would be so stupid as to turn the power off?

Ahead of her, Krynter was obviously thinking worse thoughts.

'Oh Christ,' he was muttering, repeating it over and over to himself. 'What now? What now?'

Temple nearly walked up to him then, if only to cuff him around the head and tell him to pull himself together. She restrained herself. She still wanted to see what he planned on doing; revealing herself now would achieve nothing.

For a few moments she thought he was going to turn around and run back to his lab. Finally, he summoned up the courage, flicked on a torch and continued towards the compost heap.

Temple followed.

HOWARD AND KIRBY ran from the stables, the sound of cracking walls and Gregor's screams (Howard tried to pretend they were *only* Gregor's screams) following them into the trees.

'I need to find Hubcap,' Howard said, turning around and trying to get his bearings. 'I don't suppose you know where he might be?'

'No idea, they marched me from the car straight into that room, same as you.'

'There must be a main building or something?'

'You're in Kew Gardens, there's *lots* of main buildings. We should just get out of here.'

Howard stared at her. 'Go if you want, obviously it's up to you, but I'm not leaving without him.' He looked around, trying to judge where most of the light was coming from, and began heading in that direction.

For a moment, Kirby just stood still. She didn't know these people. She'd caught a lucky break escaping from the stables, a chance to get clear and put whatever this was behind her. Why should she throw all that away for the sake of a couple of kids she didn't even know?

Because they'd probably do the same for her. Maybe that wasn't a good enough reason to throw your life away, but it was the one that would bug her forever if she just turned and ran.

Frustrated to find herself as trapped by her own morals as she had been by a locked door, she ran after Howard.

'The palace is this way,' she said, feeling better if she took some control, 'who knows if that's where they take them, but it's a start.'

'Thank you.'

'It's fine. But I'm not just walking in there to get caught again. We'll take a look around, see what we can figure out and then play it from there.'

Chapter Twelve

KRYNTER APPROACHED THE compost heap slowly. He'd turned off his torch, not wanting to stand out as a target. He rolled it between his thumb and forefinger, imagining the horrors it might show in its beam if he used it.

The silhouette of the compost heap was clear enough against the night sky, a writhing mass of shadows that danced in the moonlight. He could hear the noise of crunching leaves and cracking branches and he knew he should just run. To hell with this place and to hell with Shandler. He wanted nothing to do with whatever was going on on the other side of that fence. Walking down here, he'd hoped that he'd find nothing untoward: a false alarm, a dose of panic and paranoia. But now... that silhouette was getting so big.

He should go back to the house, warn someone, get the soldiers out here with their flamethrowers and grenades. It might not be enough but it could turn the tide. The longer the plant was allowed to grow and multiply, the less chance anyone would have of stopping it.

But if he went back now, he'd be caught up in it all; they'd have him back here on the front line, Shandler demanding he do something with his hormone spray to make it effective.

He'd just leave while he still could. Yes. That was the best. Get out of here and head as far out of the city as possible. After all, in a few months there wouldn't be much of a city left. Maybe he could even get on a boat somewhere, leave the country. He'd like to see the damned plant propagate across oceans.

He backed away from the compost heap and felt something hard pressing into his back.

'You were just coming back to warn us, yes?' said Temple in his ear.

Krynter cried out in panic, turned around and stumbled, falling to the earth, the sounds of the compost heap even louder now. Could it sense them? Oh God... could it *hear* them?

'What are you doing sneaking around out here?' he

asked, trying to get back on his feet.

Temple pushed him back down with her booted foot. 'No,' she said, 'you stay right there, like the grubby, fat worm you are.'

'How dare you!' She raised her gun and he changed tack immediately. 'Of course I was coming back to the house!' he said. 'We need to get the soldiers out here to contain this thing *now*.'

'You talk to yourself,' she told him, pulling her walkie-talkie from her belt, 'you were mumbling about running away. "To hell with this place. To hell with Shandler."' She'd turned the walkie-talkie off when following Krynter, not wanting it going off and alerting him to her presence. She turned it on now and immediately started raising teams from the barracks.

Krynter wondered if this was his opportunity, might he manage to run while she was distracted? Of course not, he decided, how much concentration did someone like Temple need to shoot someone in the back? His only hope was to reassure her of his importance.

'I was just scared,' he said. 'It was a momentary thing, do you blame me? Look at it! I just panicked, that's all. Let me up, I can help deal with this. I can help fight it.'

'With your wonder spray?' she asked, sceptical. She

nudged the water pistol he'd dropped with her foot. 'Go on then,' she said, kicking it towards him.

He picked up the water pistol and got to his feet. 'Absolutely. All for one, eh?' He smiled. 'How long before the others get here?'

'Doesn't matter,' she said, shoving him towards the compost heap. 'If your chemical crap is so great, you don't need to wait for reinforcements do you?'

He stared at her and the penny slowly dropped. 'Don't be ridiculous!' he said. 'You can't expect me to go charging in alone.'

'That's exactly what I expect you to do. It's a perfect opportunity for you to stand by your work. If you've done your job properly then you've got nothing to worry about have you?'

He turned towards the compost heap, the giant, writhing silhouette even bigger now. There was the creaking sound of stretching wire as it pushed against the perimeter fence.

'I won't do it,' he said, almost to himself.

'Then I'll just shoot you here and now for desertion,' she replied, sharpening the threat by stepping closer, her gun aimed at his head.

'Bitch,' he muttered, 'stupid psychotic bitch.' He turned to look at the compost heap, water pistol in hand, and wondered how best to get out of the situation. If the chemical had some effect he could maybe get past the creature and make a run for it. Yes, if he could use the creature as cover there might be a slim chance.

He walked towards the compost heap just as the air filled with a loud snap and the twanging of wires. The fence was down. That might be to his advantage. If he'd had to go inside, he would have been trapped in there, now it was open his odds would be better.

The creature seemed to double in size as it fell outwards, great tendrils swarming out into the open, free to move. He took a couple of steps back, only too aware that Temple would be right behind him. But not for long, he thought, the closer he got the more she'd hang back, wanting to stay clear of danger.

He veered to his right, wanting to get close enough to the creature to keep Temple back but not so close he wouldn't be able to retreat.

It reared up, its thick branches drawing lines of darkness across the night sky.

'Look at you,' he said, not without a touch of awe, 'just look at what you've become.'

He looked over his shoulder as he inched around it, wanting to see where Temple was. As he'd guessed she'd held her ground, still aiming her gun at him but now far enough away that his chances of escape were growing better with every step. He kept one eye on her and one eye on the creature, water pistol raised high. If he timed it right...

The creature shuddered and he squirted the water pistol at it in panic, running around it, keeping up a steady stream of the chemical spray. The liquid hit its soft, green hide with a sound like fabric tearing. It had no effect whatsoever.

Behind him, Temple fired a couple of rounds; at him or the creature he couldn't tell. He hoped it had turned on her as well, that would be some consolation. *If I have to die today*, he decided, *I'd like it better if she did too.*

His finger depressed the trigger on an empty water pistol, pathetic bursts of air puffing from its dripping nozzle. He kept firing, beyond noticing.

He was on the far side of the compost heap by the time it caught him. He tried to stare at the open gardens ahead as he was yanked up into the air by the tendrils that had caught his ankles. *I can just about bear this*, he thought, *if I don't have to see it.* Like a child in the doctor's surgery looking away as the hypodermic needle advances, he twisted his head to stare at the trees as he felt the tension build in his groin, his legs being pulled in different directions. Finally, as he swung through the air he couldn't help but glance down at the giant plant, turned grey by the moonlight.

'To hell with you,' he said.

Then there was the sound of tearing and the splatter of something thick and wet falling on leaves.

Chapter Thirteen

HUBCAP LAY ON the operating table, completely unaware that the man he was waiting for would never arrive. It had been about twenty minutes since the soldiers had strapped him tight and wandered out, chatting about that night's meal. Hubcap hoped it gave them the squits.

'Hey!' he shouted, straining his neck to try and look behind him. 'Is there anyone out there?'

Silence.

He pulled at the straps that held his wrists but they were so tight he was getting pins and needles in his fingers; he couldn't see himself pulling free. Just to make doubly sure he had a mad five seconds thrashing around, but all it achieved was friction burns on his wrists.

He looked around the cluttered lab, not hopeful of seeing anything useful but because it beat staring up at the large lamp that hovered above him. Every work surface seemed full of junk. Chemistry equipment, empty food wrappers, sheets of paper. He spotted a scalpel on a small, portable equipment trolley but as he had yet failed to master the art of attracting metal objects with the power of his mind; he gave up on staring at it after about a minute.

'The world ends,' he said, 'everything gets weird, and I mean *everything*, but I still don't get super powers. Life sucks.'

'It can seem like that sometimes,' said a voice behind him, 'but, you know, hang on in there, things might get better.'

Hubcap twisted to look at the man behind him. He was a strange sight, dressed in priest's robes and wearing a big false beard. 'Or not,' the man shrugged, 'who knows? That's the thing with non-interventionism.'

He spoke with an American accent and was looking around the room in a daze. 'Weird dream,' he said, 'maybe it was the onions.'

'I don't suppose you could let me out of here?' Hubcap asked. 'Whoever you are.'

'I'm God,' the man replied.

'Oh yeah,' Hubcap nodded, not having the first idea how to reply to that, 'cool. So how about it? Fancy loosening a strap or two?'

'I shouldn't really,' God said, 'that's kind of the rule with being a non-interventionist deity. In fact it's probably the only rule: don't intervene.'

'Yeah, fair enough,' said Hubcap, 'but it's not a big deal is it? A couple of straps?'

'I didn't get your name?' God asked. 'I mean, obviously, being God, I know it, but let's stick to the formalities.'

'Hubcap.'

'Weird name.'

'Says the man who calls himself "God".'

Hubcap looked around to see if there was anyone else there. Maybe these guys kept a mental hospital on site or something, this bloke had certainly escaped from somewhere medical.

'It's my name,' God replied. 'I know because I gave it to myself.'

'Yeah, okay…' Hubcap had been momentarily grateful at the notion of someone else being in the room with him— someone, that is, who didn't seem intent on experimenting on him or cutting him into little pieces—but that gratitude was starting to wear off.

'I don't think I could do the straps,' God said, 'even though this is only a dream.'

'Fair enough, forget I mentioned it. Is there anyone else out there?'

God ignored the question. 'I suppose I could pass you that scalpel. Then you'd still be doing most of it on your own. Don't blame me if you cut your wrists open though. I can't stand people who won't accept their own failings.'

'What?' Hubcap had only been half listening. 'The scalpel? Yeah that would be totally cool, perfect, brilliant in fact. If you just left it near my hand I could probably manage on my own.'

God went over to the equipment trolley, picked up the scalpel and walked back over. Briefly, it occurred to Hubcap that the man might suddenly decide to stab him with it. After all, who knows what a man who thinks he's God might get up to?

God placed the scalpel carefully in Hubcap's hand. 'It's very sharp. I think you'll have to hold it carefully.'

'Don't worry,' said Hubcap, wiggling it around to try and find the best way he could cut the strap. He couldn't find an angle that worked. It always looked easy in movies. 'Ahh,' he stabbed himself in the forearm.

'I told you to be careful.' Hubcap looked over at God who was fretting with his false beard. 'I just bet you're going to end up bleeding to death and then it'll all be my fault.'

'Not your fault at all, honest,' said Hubcap, 'all on me. It was really good of you to… Oh balls!' He dropped the scalpel and it clattered on the floor. Hubcap sighed. 'I don't suppose you'd mind picking that up for me?'

'It's excruciating to watch,' said God. 'I don't think it's a very good idea.'

'It beats the alternative,' said Hubcap. 'Any minute now someone's going to come through that door and do some kind of stupid experiment on me.'

'What sort of experiment?'

'No idea. Something to do with turning plants into drugs or plants into people or people into plants… I really have no idea, I'm just trying to keep out of it all to be honest. One thing I do know, at the end of it I'll be dead so… you know… not so bothered about the stabby scalpel.'

'You can't turn people into plants,' said God, 'it's against nature.'

'I know! You know what some of these science guys get like though… there's no stopping 'em once they've had an idea is there?'

'I really don't approve,' said God. 'If I wanted people to be plants I'd have made them that way. Have these idiots not heard of bio-diversification?'

Hubcap certainly hadn't. 'Yeah, mental innit? So… about the scalpel.'

'No,' God shook his head, 'the scalpel's a bad idea.' He kicked it away with his foot. 'I'll just undo the strap. After all, one good interfere deserves another.'

'You bet,' said Hubcap as God undid the strap.

From somewhere in the distance an alarm began ringing.

'What's that?' God asked. 'These freaks are wiring their straps up to alarms now?'

'I don't think it was the strap,' said Hubcap, pulling his hand free and rolling over to undo the other strap. 'But it sounds like a good time to leave, whatever it is.'

Both hands free, he turned back to find God had gone, the room was now empty again.

'Oh shut up!' he said. 'Where'd the loon go?'

He undid the strap around his feet and got down from the table, moving over to the door. The weird guy must have gone outside, he thought. Hubcap believed in lots of things but he didn't believe in God. Even if he did, he doubted he'd believe in one who wore a false beard and had a New York accent. Never mind where the man had come from or where he'd now gone to, the important thing was to take advantage and get the hell out of there.

Chapter Fourteen

HOWARD AND KIRBY were hiding in the trees that surrounded Kew Palace when the alarms went off. The sudden noise nearly sent both of them running into the bushes in panic.

'It's not us,' said Howard, tugging on Kirby's arm.

She snatched her arm away. 'Says who? Maybe they've seen what's going on at the stables?'

'If they have then they'll have more to deal with than us, won't they? You think they're going to care about a couple of missing people when they clock what Gregor's turned into?'

Kirby thought about that for a minute and agreed he had a point. 'They're still going to be on alert though,' she said. 'I don't want to run into a bunch of twitchy soldiers armed to the teeth.'

In the distance there was the sound of people running across the grass.

'Hopefully we won't,' said Howard. 'They'll all be too busy shooting at bigger things.'

SHANDLER WAS IN the middle of one of the lawns when his radio crackled and he heard Temple's voice demanding heavily-armed units get over to the compost heap.

'Where the hell have you been?' he shouted at her through the walkie-talkie. 'And while we're on the subject, where the hell is Krynter?'

The answer to neither question pleased him.

He looked at his watch. Twenty-seven minutes until HA/HA's deadline. Damn it. The last thing he wanted to do was to give the AI's warning any credence. His pride just wouldn't stand for it. Did he even have anything capable of destroying all the chase plant matter in that time? Hit the Temperate House and the compost heap with as many incendiary bombs as they could and hope they could contain the devastation?

The Temperate House... Temple was concentrating all her troops on the compost heap, but if the plant matter there was out of control...

Shandler ran for the Temperate House, screaming orders into his walkie-talkie as he did so.

THERE WAS A small part of Gregor—a very, very small part—that was aware of what he was doing. As he dragged his constantly expanding body out of the crumbling remains of the stables, pulling himself into the fresh air, that part acknowledged that he had certainly made something of himself. He had become bigger, stronger and far more powerful than he had ever dreamed possible. A shame it had come at the cost of his humanity but, when faced with insurmountable circumstances, you just had to find the silver lining where you could.

He stretched and the feeling was not unlike the freeing of cramped muscles, a sense of finally being able to expand into the space your body needed. Behind him, someone was whimpering beneath crushed rubble; it was a wet, desperate sound, the sort of noise a dying thing makes. He ignored it. In the distance he could hear gunfire: a reassuring noise, a familiar call to action that resonated with the buried consciousness inside him. He moved towards it.

*   *   *

THOUSANDS OF MILES away, in the new, glittering neon world of post-Change Japan, HA/HA came to a decision. To say it had ruminated would have been to give it human characteristics it didn't possess. To the AI, thinking was a simple, and instant, case of arithmetic. It was a collation of facts followed by a logical outcome. Once that outcome was reached it gave no more consideration to the matter, to do so would be a waste of system resources. Why double-check your facts when you were infallible? It simply acted on the processed information and moved on to the next string of data requiring its attention. A subset of its processing took control of the matter, hacking and then conversing with dormant systems off the coast of the UK. It tested those systems, analysed their potential effectiveness and found them viable. It acted on its decision. The fact that, in this case, its decision would cause a considerable loss of human life didn't even merit acknowledgement.

Chapter Fifteen

HUBCAP SAW NO-ONE as he ran through the corridors of Kew Palace. He hung back on every corner, crept past every door, expecting a heavy hand to fall on his shoulder at any moment. The fact that one never did was almost worrying. What was going on around here that was such a big deal the place had been all but abandoned?

Opening a large pair of double doors that he hoped would lead to an exit, he instead found himself in Shandler's study. To the rear was a massive desk with a computer monitor and little else. A large, grotesquely pompous, portrait of Shandler looked down on him from the wall behind it.

'Ego, much?' Hubcap muttered, about to turn around when he spotted something on a coffee table to the right of the desk. It was Shandler's phone.

'Might as well,' Hubcap decided, grabbing it and putting it in his pocket. After all, when the soldiers had snatched them away from the car park, he'd left his iPad behind. That meant this guy owed him some tech, as far as Hubcap was concerned.

Stepping back out into the corridor he carried on in search of the front door.

HOWARD AND KIRBY were creeping up towards the main door of the palace, cautiously peering through the windows into empty, opulent rooms.

'Place seems empty,' said Howard.

In the distance there was the sound of automatic gunfire and breaking glass. Their captors clearly had lots of problems to deal with. Howard could only hope they continued. He gestured towards the noise. 'Sounds like Gregor's causing trouble.'

'I don't know,' Kirby looked out across the gardens. 'Sounds to me like the noise is coming from a couple of different directions. Whatever's happening I think it's more than just Gregor.'

'Good,' said Howard, 'anything that keeps them busy.'

They moved towards the front door, just in time for

Hubcap to come bursting out of it, terrifying them both.

'Hello you two,' he said. 'I got bored waiting for you to rescue me so I thought I'd see if you needed rescuing instead.'

In the distance, a plume of fire lit up the darkness.

'Let's just get out of here,' said Kirby, 'before we got caught up in whatever this mess is.'

'Can you remember the way out from when you came here with the school?' Howard asked Hubcap.

'Not really,' Hubcap admitted. 'How about we just run like hell in the opposite direction to all the fighting?'

'Wait,' said Kirby, 'I just had a better idea.'

BY THE TIME Shandler reached the Temperate House, the parent plant had already demolished the roof. Pressing on the walls from the inside, glass was shattering and wood splitting as it swelled beyond the ancient building's confines.

'Too far,' Shandler said. 'Whole damn mess has gone too far.'

The feeling was utterly alien to him, swinging from being completely in control of his situation to swamped by chaos.

'Burn the whole thing!' he shouted as a troop of soldiers arrived behind him. 'No choice now, destroy it before it gets out of hand.'

Who am I kidding? he wondered as the soldiers began lobbing incendiary grenades towards the creature. *It got out of hand long ago.* If he could at least wipe this monstrosity out… Maybe then he could get back on his feet, write this whole thing off as more trouble than it had been worth. If he could convince the rest of The Hellfire Club that he'd made the decision off his own back, rather than as a desperate response to the mess that now surrounded him… Yes. It didn't matter what you did, what mattered was how you *appeared* to do it.

The Temperate House erupted in flames, the writhing, expanding thing inside it pushing the last of the toppling structure away as the fire began to catch. Would it be enough? Would the fire control it? What about the mess at the compost heap? Could Temple handle that?

The ground around Shandler and the soldiers began to move, the grass rippling, the earth spraying upwards, trees toppling with screams of creaking wood.

Shandler fell backwards as the ground he'd been stood on was peeled back by the roots beneath, tearing upwards and lashing out at the plant's attackers.

The light of the flames showed the destruction near the blazing ruins of the Temperate House, well-cut lawns and herbaceous borders turned into gaping craters and mounds of displaced soil the size of outbuildings. But beyond the light there was the sound of tearing vegetation and a steady rain of dirt and rocks. Shandler had severely underestimated how big this thing had grown. How far did these roots stretch? How mammoth was the thing?

Shandler had built a fortune on snap decisions, on judging the odds and steering his business accordingly. Initially this had been working the stock market, then it had been second-guessing consumer trends and technological innovations. Now it was a simpler affair: he looked at the warzone Kew Gardens had become and the likelihood of HA/HA's prediction hit home.

'Throw everything you've got at it!' he shouted, getting to his feet and retreating as fast as he could. 'Reinforcements are on the way.'

As he ran he spoke into his walkie-talkie. 'Temple? What's your status?'

TEMPLE'S STATUS WAS not good. She'd allowed half of her limited compliment of men to meet Shandler at the

Temperate House even though she knew that all she would achieve was splitting her meagre resources on two fronts so they could be soundly beaten on both.

Shandler's private army had been impressive enough when all it had to do was strong-arm a few packs of looters or take on small sproutling outbreaks. In those situations it had been like squashing a fly with a mallet. Now, looking up at the massive, continually re-forming and swelling plant creature as it pulled itself towards them, she realised her and her men had become the flies.

When her employer's voice spoke to her from the walkie-talkie clipped on her belt she ignored it. She'd just detailed ten men—half of her current compliment—to lay down a defensive fire break between them and the creature, petrol poured in a wide arc then lit. She had no great hope of it being useful but she'd run out of incendiary grenades after two failed volleys. Fire was the only thing that really achieved anything. Their bullets, when concentrated enough, bought them time as they cut and minced the "limbs" of their opponent, but the plant regrew so quickly that all they were really doing was throwing away ammunition.

The creature dragged itself onto the flaming barrier. *How is it doing that?* she wondered. She was used to the sproutlings walking, after all, they were human once, but this thing? How did a plant uproot itself and crawl along the ground? Just another chunk of impossibility in this world she had fought to survive in.

'Spray the rest of the petrol!' she shouted, her men dousing the creature with the supply they had left, desperately hoping they could get the thing to catch alight. It did, for all the good it seemed to do; its heavy, almost fluid mass, beating at itself and rolling in the earth where the flames soon extinguished.

Chapter Sixteen

'Kirby I love you,' said Hubcap, 'and I mean that in a very real and physical way.'

They were stood outside a large garage, Kirby was just inside the door, beating on a metal cabinet with a large rock. She paused.

'I will punch you so hard if you say another word,' she told him, returning to the cabinet.

Hubcap opened his mouth and then closed it again. He believed her. He turned back to the large SUV Kirby had led them to.

'You really know how to drive it?' Howard asked.

There was a clatter as the cabinet opened.

'Yes, I really know how to drive it,' she replied. 'What's the licence number?'

Hubcap read it out, eager to be helpful in the sort of way that might not get him a punch in the mouth.

'Got it,' she said, snatching a set of keys and pointing them at the car. She pressed the button that controlled the locks and there was a bleep and a loud clunk as it opened. 'So?' she stared at them. 'Get in!'

'I can drive too,' said Hubcap, 'Tiger taught me.' Kirby stared at him. 'Not saying I want to!' he told her, holding his hands up in surrender. 'Just mentioning it that's all.' He let Howard take the passenger seat; he felt safer in the back, out of Kirby's range.

Kirby started the engine, turned on the headlights and pulled out aggressively enough that both Howard and Hubcap were thrown back in their seats.

'I still don't really know where we're going,' she admitted, 'but if we follow the road we should get somewhere that isn't here eventually.'

'Whatever,' said Hubcap, 'you see the outside of this thing? I reckon we could drive through a whole platoon of those guys and come out laughing.'

They turned a corner and their headlights fell on something that blocked their entire front view: the mutated form of Gregor, dragging himself towards the distant fighting. Kirby slammed on the brakes. Gregor paused. While he no longer seemed to possess anything recognisable as a head, several of his tendrils and the fat nodules that covered his lumpen body turned towards them.

'Oh God...' Kirby sighed. 'I'm reversing.'

'Wait,' said Howard, thinking back to how the soldiers had handled Gregor way back when they'd been captured in the supermarket carpark. He looked around him. 'How do you open the window?'

'You want to open the window?' shouted Hubcap. 'Are you mad?'

Kirby pressed the button that wound the passenger window down and Hubcap leaned out, the thing that had been Gregor now, slowly, shifting towards them.

'Soldier!' Howard shouted. 'Clear the way! Priority order, soldier! Move it!'

Gregor paused again, the surface of his body writhing in what could have been either confusion or hunger; Howard wouldn't like to bet on which. He tried again, shouting even louder, trying to make his voice as aggressive and authoritative as possible. 'Now soldier! On the double!'

Inside the creature, the fading consciousness of Gregor was electric at the sound of these words. This was non-negotiable. This was the word of God. If a soldier knows one thing it's to follow orders. The rest of him, the plant that was drowning his humanity, wanted to go over there and crush and tear and kill but Gregor fought back. They had to carry on towards the sound of gunfire, they had to follow orders.

Slowly—there was so much of it, it could hardly move any other way—it turned away from the SUV and continued across the track, moving down towards the distant glow of flames and the sound of screaming.

As soon as it was clear, Kirby stamped on the accelerator and they moved forward again.

'That was actually brilliant,' said Hubcap. 'I'm genuinely impressed by you back here.'

'It was nothing,' said Howard with a smile.

There was a buzzing sound.

'Was that a phone?' Kirby asked, leaning forward to try to get an idea of where they were going. 'Are you actually being texted on an actual phone?'

'Not mine,' Hubcap admitted. 'I picked it up in the house, nice bit of kit.' He pulled the phone out of his pocket and held it up. 'See? Nice.' He looked at the screen. 'It's a message from some guy called HAHA... weird name, auto-correct probably, I hate auto-correct, it always makes my... Oh.'

'What?' asked Howard.

'We need to get away from here fast,' said Hubcap. 'Seriously Kirby, put your foot down!'

LAST CHANCE, TEMPLE thought, as the helicopter banked above them.

'Get clear!' she shouted, then gave the order into her walkie-talkie.

An air to ground missile shot towards the creature but Temple didn't even have a fraction of a second to hope it would make the difference. A thick tendril batted it out of the air, sending it off target, where it blew up in an explosion of light and noise.

The helicopter banked again, lining up for a second shot. A pair of tendrils shot upwards and wrapped themselves around it, the sound of the pilot's panic distorting through the small speaker in Temple's radio.

'Fire again!' she shouted, knowing that, whatever happened the pilot was dead now anyway, if they could at least deal a wounding blow to the creature in the process.

The helicopter was whipped down towards her and her few remaining men. They panicked, scattering in multiple directions as the helicopter was hammered into the ground, its rotor blades hurling great chunks of earth skyward before they crumpled and snapped off.

This is it, Temple thought, *this is the moment where it all becomes pointless. Nothing we do can win this anymore. Sometimes you face a situation in battle where you have only two choices left to you: run or die.*

'Withdraw!' she shouted, turning to find herself facing the swollen remains of Gregor Tobanek.

It rolled right over her, utterly unaware that the sound of snapping and splintering beneath it was anything more than breaking branches.

SHANDLER LOOKED AT his watch as he ran. A little over ten minutes before HA/HA's deadline. He needed to get clear of the entire site, take stock and then, if need be, wipe the entire place from the surface of the planet. The AI had suggested that the chase would kill him, that he'd die unless he destroyed it. Well, he'd just have to deal with being wrong, wouldn't he? If that was the only victory Shandler could pull out of this mess, he'd be happy with it.

He'd get to the garage, grab the fastest vehicle he could and put some distance between him and...

A pair of headlights suddenly fixed on him as he crossed

the road, one of the military SUVs tearing along at high speed. Was that one of his men? Was it Krynter? Temple? The headlights blinded him as the car hit, hurling him into an overgrown rose bush by the side of the road. He tried to turn his head to watch it vanish on its way towards the main exit but something had broken inside him and his body wasn't responding as it should. He was thankful for that in a small way; he was sure he should be in a lot more pain than he actually was.

'YOU CAN'T JUST leave him!' Howard was shouting, reaching for the wheel.

'You just watch me,' said Kirby. 'If he was to do with this lot he deserves whatever's coming to him, I'm not going to risk dying over it.'

Howard twisted in his seat, trying to look through the rear window at the man they'd hit. It was too late, they were going so fast there was no longer any sign of him.

Kirby pressed even harder on the accelerator as one of the main exits appeared ahead, pulling out onto the road beyond. As they'd hoped, while many local roads were still clogged with abandoned vehicles, the roads around Kew had been cleared to allow the soldiers room to move.

She turned left, aiming for the A4, driving as fast as she could.

'How long?' she shouted to Hubcap.

'Erm...' He checked the message in the phone. 'Four minutes.'

'Four minutes,' she repeated, 'let's hope it's enough.'

THE PLANTS WERE fusing, both of them coming together by branch, tendril and root. The union felt like strength, it felt like a new beginning for the species as the best genetic traits of each merged together to form the single, dominant plant. A plant that would then go on to self-seed in its own image, spread further and further into new soil, new habitat, new feeding grounds...

It didn't notice the noise in the sky above it, wasn't aware of the significance of the whoosh of air. It was as close as a plant gets to euphoria, right up until the night sky turned bright and Kew burned.

SHANDLER HEARD THE noise of the missile but couldn't know what it meant. If he'd only kept his phone on him he would have received the warning from HA/HA, would have known that it had accessed the onboard computer of a derelict submarine off the south coast and hacked its launch codes. He would have known, in short, that that almost gentle hiss of air signified a small warhead being delivered directly into the heart of his current location.

Who's whispering? he wondered, the thorns from the rose bush tearing into him as he sank further and further into its branches.

Then the sky was full of light and fire and nobody was whispering any more.

BY THE TIME the missile hit, Howard, Hubcap and Kirby were two miles away and counting, Kirby still pushing forward at the very limit of the SUV's engine. She feathered the brakes as the light burst in the sky behind them, wanting to make sure she had full control in case they were still close enough for the shockwave to hit.

The effect was brief: a flash of light, spreading out over the clouds like dye dropped into water, then dropping back. In the distance, Kew burned, deep red, fringed with warm orange. If it had been day they would have seen the wave of dust and debris pushed out from the epicentre of the explosion. If the roar of the engine wasn't so loud they would have heard the crunch and rumble, the spread of noise working its way across the streets and parkland. As it was, saved by distance and darkness, the event seemed almost anti-climactic. An incendiary full stop to their night.

Kirby slowed down but didn't stop, what was the point? They may as well put as much distance between themselves and the explosion.

'So,' she asked, her voice ridiculously casual, 'where are we heading now?'